ROBIN HOOD

SHERIFF GOT YOUR TONGUE?

D0177431

BBC CHILDREN'S BOOKS

Published by the Penguin Group
Penguin Books Ltd, 80 Strand, London WC2R 0RL, England
Penguin Group (USA) Inc., 375 Hudson Street, New York, New York 10014, USA
Penguin Group (Australia) Ltd, 250 Camberwell Road, Camberwell, Victoria, 3124, Australia
(a division of Pearson Australia Group Pty Ltd)
Canada, India, New Zealand, South Africa

Published by BBC Children's Books, 2006

10 9 8 7 6 5 4 3 2 1

ISBN 978 1 405 90319 6

Printed in the United Kingdom

ROBIN HOOD

SHERIFF GOT YOUR TONGUE?

Adapted by Kay Woodward from the television script "Sheriff Got Your Tongue?" by Dominic Minghella for the television series Robin Hood created by Dominic Minghella and Foz Allan for Tiger Aspect as shown on BBC One.

CHAPTER ONE

The Sheriff of Nottingham was not having a good day. Not only had four petty criminals slipped through his fingers, but Robin of Locksley, Earl of Huntingdon – the crusading lord turned common outlaw – had outwitted him too. Robin had made him look a fool. And *nobody* made the Sheriff look a fool.

Nobody.

The villagers risked stealthy glances at the Sheriff and his men as they marched into Locksley village. The Sheriff was a familiar – if unwelcome – figure clad in luxurious fur-lined robes that were so much warmer than the villagers' attire. Spotting his angry, red face, one man couldn't help smirking, before quickly turning away. Too late. He'd been seen.

The Sheriff leaned towards his faithful

2

supporter, Guy of Gisborne. 'Find out that man's name,' he hissed.

Within minutes, the people of Locksley were assembled in the village square, facing the Sheriff and his evil henchmen. The villagers knew this visit meant trouble. They'd all heard of Robin's daring plan to snatch the prisoners from the gallows – news travelled fast in Nottingham. Now, the atmosphere was heavy with fear.

At last, the Sheriff spoke. 'I have come to visit Robin of Locksley, but find him…' he paused to feign surprise, '…not at home. Perhaps one of you would like to inform me of his whereabouts? He and I need to have a little… conversation.' The words were laden with menace.

The villagers darted uneasy glances at each other, shifting uncomfortably where they stood.

'Nobody knows, nobody knows…' chanted the Sheriff. 'Then there's a little reward.' He produced a leather purse. 'Shall we say twenty pounds…?' Listening delightedly to the murmurs of his reluctant audience, he added, 'And then *somebody* knows…' He smiled arrogantly, with the confident air of someone who is used to getting his own way.

Nobody said a word.

Guy of Gisborne suddenly lost his cool. 'Loosen your tongues or lose your tongues!' he snapped, his expression cold and hard. His hand moved towards the hefty broadsword that hung at his side.

The Sheriff rolled his eyes at Gisborne's clumsy outburst.

But still nobody spoke.

Gisborne looked to the Sheriff for permission – it was granted. And, protesting wildly, the villager who had dared to smile earlier was dragged from the crowd.

'Cut out his tongue,' drawled the Sheriff of Nottingham, as if this whole affair were too boring for words. Menacingly, he scissored his fingers across his own tongue, as if the words weren't clear enough. 'One an hour until somebody talks.'

The villager was held tightly by one of the Sheriff's men, while another advanced, wielding a pair of huge, vicious-looking pincers. Wearing an expression of grim intent, he forced the medieval tool into the terrified man's mouth.

There was a long, bloodcurdling scream.

Will Scarlett stopped dead in his tracks. He'd expected to find Robin and the others gathered around the campfire, cooking a mouth-watering meal of spit-roasted rabbit. But as he peered through the lush, green foliage of Sherwood Forest, he saw something altogether different.

The rabbit was roasting all right. But rather than warming themselves around the flickering flames, Robin, Much and Allan A Dale were bound roughly to nearby trees, stripped to the waist. From his leafy hiding place, Will couldn't identify the four assailants. So, keeping his distance and staying well out of sight, he tracked around the edge of the clearing to get a better look.

Leaning casually against his tree trunk, Robin

wore an expression of utter calm. He looked for all the world as if he were captured every day of the week and that, really, it was no big deal because he would have escaped long before the campfire died anyway.

Much was more agitated. 'You're making a mistake,' he said, watching as the youngest attacker checked their purses and coat pockets for money.

Roy had heard it all before. 'What?' he said irritably. 'Are you going to send an army to hunt us down and tear us limb from limb? Do you think we're frightened of the Sheriff?' He turned to the giant of a man who watched from beyond the campfire – by far the most imposing of the captors. 'We, frightened?' he demanded.

The giant, Little John, shook his head and grunted, 'No.'

Much tried again. 'No,' he said patiently. 'We also are against the Sheriff.'

'What do you want?' sneered Roy. 'A medal?'

Little John reached towards the fire and plucked the rabbit from the flames. Without waiting for it to cool, he tore hungrily at the flesh with his teeth.

'We should be on the same side,' continued Much, growing more and more worried by the second. 'We should – Master, tell him!'

Robin shrugged, but refused to speak.

At that moment, the sight of the hot rabbit meat disappearing into Little John's cavernous mouth distracted Much. 'I think you'll find that is not yet cooked,' he said.

Little John carried on eating.

'I think you'll find he eats them raw,' said Hanton, another of the outlaws.

'Raw?' asked Much anxiously. 'Is that wise? That is *dangerous.*'

'Oooh…' said Roy, totally unfazed. 'You a noble?' he said to Robin.

Robin paused for a moment before replying. 'Yes and no.'

Forrest, the fourth outlaw, sniffed deeply. 'Smells like one,' he said. 'Smells really lovely.

Like flowers. Lavender.'

'Rose petals,' corrected Much, thinking longingly of the petal-strewn bath he'd enjoyed during his brief stay at Locksley Manor. It didn't look like they'd be returning to Robin's ancestral home any time soon. Not after their fight with the Sheriff of Nottingham and his men.

'What?' Forrest interrupted Much's daydream. 'You rub it on, do you? Lavender balm?' He sniffed again. 'You smell too.'

Much set the record straight. 'No, I had a bath. *He* washed with rose petals.'

'And they reckon they're serfs?' Hanton said scornfully to his fellow outlaws. 'Think about it. Know any serfs who take lavender baths?'

'No,' said Roy. 'John?'

Little John, who was still busy eating, shook his head.

'It's *not* lavender,' insisted Much, fit to burst with frustration.

While everyone bickered, Robin scanned the clearing with the practised eye of an archer.

And not just any old archer. Robin of Locksley had taken part in the king's crusade for five long years. He'd fought in the most bloodthirsty of battles, witnessing unmentionable suffering. He'd cheated death – and he'd killed too. And now, Robin knew the importance of keeping alert. So it was hardly surprising that he instantly spotted Will Scarlett, hidden among the foliage. When Will held up his knife, he shook his head. Now was not the time to fight back.

Triumphantly, Forrest produced a small semi-circle of metal from Allan A Dale's pocket. 'Got a ha'penny here, John,' he said.

This got Robin's attention. 'You have the horses,' he said firmly. 'Leave him his ha'penny.'

'How come you've got no purse?' asked Roy, curious now.

'I was not planning to be in the woods,' said Robin. He turned awkwardly, angling his head towards Little John. 'Is this what you do? Stealing willy-nilly?'

'Stealing willy-nilly?' mimicked Roy. Puzzled

by the words, he frowned at the big man. 'Know what he's saying?'

Robin sighed heavily. 'Do you care who you steal from?' he said.

Little John snorted, while Roy looked even more confused.

There was no other choice but for Robin to spell it out. 'My friend here has but a ha'penny,' he explained. 'What you take may be all he has.'

'It *is* all I have,' spluttered Allan.

'Heartbreaking,' said Roy. 'Do we care?'

Little John shook his head in reply.

'We don't care,' confirmed Roy.

'We're dead men,' Forrest said to the prisoners. 'Think about it. Outlaws.'

'That *is* sophisticated.' Robin was unimpressed.

'Big words,' sneered Roy. 'Scary!'

Little John had had enough of this squabbling. He silenced his men with a single look and gestured to signal their departure. Wordlessly, the others obeyed and in a flurry of stolen hoof beats, they were gone.

Only now did Robin look to their hidden ally. At once, Will broke cover, running to free Much and Allan. But Robin simply walked away from his tree, tossing away the rope that had tied him. Allan and Will watched in disbelief.

Much hung his head, muttering to himself. 'Those were horrible men. For all they knew we could have died here. If they had not taken our weapons, I would say we should chase after them and give them a hiding – a hiding to remember…' His voice trailed away as he too suddenly realised that Robin had freed himself. 'But how…?' he said, totally flummoxed. 'You – you let me think… If you had untied yourself, why didn't you fight?'

'I thought it better to wait,' said his friend.

'*Why*?' asked Much.

'Because you are right,' replied Robin. 'We should teach them a lesson.' He turned to the others. 'Gentlemen?'

There was an unmistakeable glint in Robin's eye, one that Much knew well – and one that he feared too. He had an awful feeling that Robin had a plan. A dangerous plan.

'Oh no, master,' he pleaded. 'Surely not…?'

Robin nodded.

Oh yes.

CHAPTER TWO

The outlaws were enjoying a celebratory meal. It had been a successful day and as if to prove it, the spoils of their thievery lay scattered all around. Robin's horses were tethered nearby, nibbling at the soft, green grass that carpeted the clearing.

Forrest chewed thoughtfully, passing a hunk of meat to Little John.

'I think you'll find that's not properly cooked!' mimicked Roy, with a snigger.

There was half-hearted chortling from Hanton and Forrest, but something had disturbed Little John, who was listening intently. He looked all round, examining the dark undergrowth for enemies.

Nothing.

Then, as an unwelcome thought suddenly

occurred to him, he looked up. Sure enough, staring right back down at him was Robin of Locksley – his arrow ready to fly. He wasn't alone. Crouched among the branches were the two other captives and a fourth man – each wielding a bow and arrow.

'It's our forest too, I think you'll find,' said Much gleefully.

Robin didn't have time for pleasantries. 'Take off your clothes,' he commanded, before dropping softly to the ground. Much, Will and Allan followed.

Swiftly, Allan A Dale snatched a length of rope from the ground and went to tie up the outlaws. But Little John was having none of it. Pushing Allan out of the way, he launched himself at their ringleader. Robin was ready, smiling as the huge man thundered towards him. At the last moment, he stepped sideways, nimbly twisted round and stuck out his foot. Little John tripped and crashed to the ground, where Robin was upon him in an instant, wrenching his arm up behind him, yanking it almost to breaking point.

Little John roared in pain, but the thick trees deadened the sound.

Guy of Gisborne and the Sheriff of Nottingham sat and waited. And waited.

The villagers stood and waited. And waited.

'Tick tock, tick tock,' muttered the Sheriff to Gisborne.

A manservant arrived with a tray, on which were balanced two ornate goblets, brimming with ruby liquid.

'Have I told you I cannot taste wine?' drawled the Sheriff. 'I have the best, of course, but I do not have the palate.' He shrugged, took the goblet anyway and gulped from it.

Quickly, Gisborne did the same.

In another part of Locksley village, two of Gisborne's men were making a very important delivery. Struggling under the weight, they unloaded grand furniture from a cart and lugged it towards Locksley Manor. There was lavish bedding too, the fabric emblazoned with the

Gisborne coat-of-arms. The heraldic colours were shockingly bright – they spoke of a man who was desperate to be noticed.

Thornton, Robin's housekeeper, was deeply unhappy at the invasion. 'This is unacceptable!' he blustered. 'My master… when this dispute is resolved… Robin will return, he will…'

'Robin?' The larger man was dismissive. 'He'll never be master of anywhere now.'

'Master of Sherwood, maybe!' said his workmate.

'Robin of the woods,' the first man quipped. He grabbed one end of a large wardrobe and together they hoisted it high.

'I like that,' said the shorter man. 'Robin of the wood.' Then he had an even better idea. 'Robin Wood!'

It was bound to catch on.

The tables had turned. Now it was the outlaws who were stripped to the waist. Much, Will and Allan set about tying them up, while Robin retrieved their possessions from the thieves' haul.

'You are… *revolting*, you know that?' said Much, his lip curling with distaste. 'My master and I fought for five years in the Holy Land – for what? So people like you could run amok with your… with your lawlessness and your disgusting, your snide… your snide… your…'

Roy winced as the rope was pulled tighter. 'Your snide, your snide?' he said mockingly.

Robin wasn't putting up with this. He threw a lazy glance in their direction. 'Dance,' he said.

'You what?'

'Dance.'

'No way,' said Roy.

Casually, Robin turned away, picked up his weapon and fired an arrow up and over his shoulder. Roy yelped as the arrow nicked his toe.

'Dance,' repeated Robin. The tone of his voice brooked no argument.

Without further complaint, the outlaw began to hop from one foot to the other. Robin unleashed more arrows at the others' feet, encouraging them to join in.

Much watched with growing delight. 'Very good,' he said happily. 'Like dancing bears.'

But Robin was genuinely furious. 'How does it feel?' he raged at the ridiculous group. 'You treat your fellow man like an *animal*. You take from people worse off than yourselves. Then you leave them to *die*? How does it *feel*?'

'Alright,' mumbled Forrest. 'You have made your point.'

The dancing petered out. But Robin's rage did not.

'Call yourselves Englishmen?' he roared. 'You are not the England we fought for. Men who think it is a *boast* to be "dead". What do you think you are doing robbing *him*...' he gestured towards Allan A Dale, 'when the Sheriff over there is robbing us all twenty times over? Skulking in the woods while *he* steals spirits and livelihoods?'

With an angry glare, Roy threw the last question back at Robin.

'Why are *you* skulking in the woods? What

are *you* going to do about it?'

Robin paused before replying. And in that brief moment, he knew what he was going to do about it. Deep down, he supposed that he'd known all along. 'Stop him,' he said firmly. 'I am going to stop him.'

'You cannot stop a sheriff.' Roy was scornful. 'Only the *crown* can withdraw his licence.'

But Robin had an answer for this, too. 'When the King returns, the Sheriff will have his comeuppance. Until then, we will scupper his sadistic punishments. We will take his *insane* taxes and give them back to the poor, where they belong.' The more he spoke, the surer he became that what he was proposing was the right thing to do. '*We* will rob *him*.'

'Sure,' said Roy.

Robin turned to the other outlaws. 'And if you "dead" men had had spines in your backs, that is what *you* would have been doing for the last five years.'

There was a brief silence, while the outlaws looked at each other.

Roy sneered. 'Rousing, Lavender Boy,' he said.

'Good luck,' was Forrest's off-hand reply.

'See you,' added Hanton.

Robin did not appreciate their tone. Didn't these idiots realise what was at stake here? Didn't they want to do the right thing? He felt his hackles rise in anger and, quick as a flash, whipped his bow to eye-level, aiming it at Roy.

'That would be a mistake,' said Roy. Laughing, he tagged on Much's catchphrase, 'I think you'll find.'

'You are in no position to argue, dunderhead,' said Much.

Robin hesitated – and in that moment he heard a telltale rustling behind him. They had company. He peered over his shoulder to see that the trees were *alive* with outlaws. There were forty or more, descending on the clearing from all sides, weapons at the ready. Robin did the only thing he could reasonably do under the circumstances. He put down his bow.

He would live to fight another day. This wasn't the time for heroics.

'Oh,' said Much, spotting the visitors too. The outlaws moved towards them. Their expressions were murderous, their arrows sharp. 'Listen,' he said, panicking now, 'you have tied *us* up. We have tied *you* up. We could call it quits. We could all be on our way.'

With a few deft tugs, the outlaws freed the four captives from the ropes that bound them.

Little John, whose ropes had been particularly tight, angrily shook the blood back into his arms. He scowled menacingly at Robin. 'Him, I do not like,' he muttered.

'It is mutual,' said Robin, returning the favour.

One of the new arrivals reached up to whisper in Little John's ear. Surprised at what he heard, the big man looked directly at Robin.

'You Robin of Locksley?' he demanded.

Robin nodded.

'Robin, Earl of Huntingdon?'

He nodded again.

'Good,' said Little John. And with that, he swung his massive fist, slamming it into Robin's face.

Everything went black.

CHAPTER THREE

'At least have the courtesy to untie him,' pleaded Much.

Little John ignored the request, instead splashing water on Robin's unconscious face. He came to with a start, blinking the drips from his eyelashes. Once again, his hands were bound firmly behind his back. Robin sighed. This was starting to get horribly repetitive. He looked up to see that Much, Allan A Dale and Will Scarlett were also captive. Then his bleary eyes clocked other, familiar sights: the run-down cottages; the towering oak tree that hung over him; the emerald beauty of the nearby forest. He knew where they were all right.

'Locksley?' he exclaimed. 'You've brought us *home*?'

'It seems there may be a reward,' Much

informed him.

The outlaws sniggered nastily.

'Twenty pounds,' said Forrest.

Roy took charge. 'You take them down,' he told Forrest. Gesturing towards Much, Allan and Will, he added, 'See if you can get something for this rabble too.'

'Me?' said Forrest, looking surprised. 'I'm supposed to be dead.'

'Me too,' said Roy crossly. 'But they won't recognise *you*.'

Forrest wasn't happy about this. 'If they do, I'll be hanged,' he said, appealing to their leader instead. 'John?'

Roy spoke slowly and clearly, as if to a dimwit. 'John can't go, can he? If they're going to recognise anyone, it's going to be John.'

It was true. Little John was the tallest man here. In a crowd, he would stand head and shoulders – and quite possibly elbows too – above everyone else. Now, he towered above them all, his huge bulk blotting out the weak afternoon sun.

'We all go,' said Little John firmly.

A bell tolled, its doleful chime echoing around Locksley as the Sheriff and Gisborne returned to the waiting crowd. The villagers still stood there, some swaying with fatigue now.

'*Another* hour,' said Gisborne. He let out a bored sigh, before addressing the crowd. 'This is not necessary. Where is Robin?'

There was silence.

'Talk!' he commanded.

Silence.

Gisborne tried another tack, his voice by turn wheedling, persuasive, sly. 'He will never be your master again. You need have no fear of reprisal from him.' He spoke the next words proudly. 'I am your master now – for good.'

This too failed to win a response from the villagers, so the Sheriff tried his luck instead. 'It is unfortunate,' he said sadly. 'A man goes to war. His spirit can be damaged, his vision blurred... and his understanding of law and order. I have even heard that there are camps in the Holy

Land, where a man is taught to hate his own land, to return there and wreak havoc and destruction.' He paused, allowing the words to sink in. 'Perhaps that has happened to Robin – we do not know. What we *do* know is that your former master did not, as the romantic among you might think, strike a blow for freedom. Make no mistake. He perverted the course of justice and in doing so he attacked the very fabric of our state. The state we all work for. The state we all pay our taxes for. He would rob us of that – our hard work and taxes.'

The Sheriff rocked back on his heels and looked around at the villagers as he spoke. He could not believe that he was wasting these words of common sense and his time, on these filthy, ungrateful people, who showed no sign of being moved by his speech. He looked around again and waited.

But the villagers continued their stubborn silence.

Clenching his fists with fury, Gisborne flashed a questioning look at the Sheriff. He replied with a curt nod.

Grimly, Gisborne's men set about their grisly task, dragging a woman at random from the crowd. She let out a terrified scream, as the menacing pincers loomed closer.

From his vantage point at the edge of the village, Little John stared. 'Oh…' was all he could say. 'Oh.'

The others watched with equal horror. None of them had ever come across something so barbaric – not even in war.

'That is nasty,' announced Much, who looked as if he might throw up. 'That is brutish. That is…'

'That is Alice,' finished Little John.

'Alice?'

'My wife.'

Heads swung round to stare at Little John. Suddenly, his huge frame seemed smaller, as if an invisible weight were crushing him.

'Thought she lived in Nottingham,' said a puzzled Forrest.

Will was incredulous. 'You're *Alice's* John?'

he asked, as realisation dawned. 'She thought you were dead – hanged at Loughborough. She searched for you…'

'I was hanged at Loughborough too,' said Roy chattily. 'Or was it Peterborough?' He peered towards the woman, who was now flailing wildly in her attempt to get away. 'Is that her?' he asked, obviously impressed. 'Nice. A looker. You never said.'

Alice let out a piercing shriek – an ear-splitting sound that jolted Little John into action. The big man picked up Robin as if he weighed no more than a bag of feathers and slung him over his shoulder.

'No!' pleaded Roy.

'I'll tear out more than their tongues…' Little John muttered.

Roy grabbed at his leader's arm. 'They'll arrest you,' he said urgently. 'You'll *hang.*'

'There is no need,' said Robin from atop the man mountain. 'It's me they want.' His tone was even and he sounded deadly serious. 'I will stop this.'

'You're not going to give *yourself* in, are you?' Roy was both scornful and disbelieving.

Robin nodded.

Much didn't like the sound of this self-sacrifice, not at all. It was by far the worst plan his master had ever come up with – and goodness knows, he'd dreamt up some corkers on the battlefield. He clutched hold of Robin's hand. 'Master, no…'

'Untie me,' said Robin.

'No, tie him up!' Suddenly Much didn't want his master to be free. He was clearly not in possession of a sane mind.

Another scream, more terrified than the last, reached their ears and Robin reacted immediately. '*Untie me!*' he ordered. 'My bow – quickly!'

Little John hesitated.

'I am good with a bow.' Robin spoke slowly and firmly. They didn't have much time. He had to act now.

But still Little John didn't give in.

'Trust me,' said Robin.

33

These words had the desired effect. Little John dropped his shoulder, letting his captive slide to the ground. Quickly, he untied him, while Roy fumbled among the stolen goods, eventually finding what he sought and tossing them in Robin's direction.

Robin's fingers closed around his trusty bow, catching the arrows with his free hand. He smiled. Now they were in business.

Meanwhile, John's wife was becoming hysterical – she retched, gasping for air. 'Help! Help me…!' One of the Sheriff's men held her head, while another took hold of her tongue, silencing her cries instantly. The pincers gripped Alice's tongue, the cold metal biting deeper and deeper into warm flesh, until…

Whoosh!

35

CHAPTER FOUR

O ut of nowhere, an arrow appeared, flying straight and true towards its target. It struck the pincers, sending them soaring. A second arrow collided with the pincers in mid-air, dividing the deadly tool into its two parts. They clattered uselessly to the ground.

Alice stared in amazement, while an excited murmuring spread through the crowd like wildfire. *It was Robin! Robin of Locksley!*

'He's here,' muttered the Sheriff under his breath. His thin lips curled into an evil smile as he turned to Gisborne. 'Find him,' he said.

As soon as he'd fired the arrows, Robin ducked back out of sight. 'God speed,' he said to the others. Briefly hugging Much, he addressed him directly. 'You have served me well, my friend, and I have led you to this.' His voice was filled with regret. 'Apologies.'

'No,' protested Much. 'Master… where are you…'

'Go.' Robin's response was kind, but firm. 'I will find a way through this.'

Much hung his head. 'The Sheriff will *hang* you,' he whispered.

Robin ran his eyes over the mixture of friends and enemies facing him. 'If he does, at least I will not die a "dead" man,' he said, singling Roy and Little John out for particularly hard stares. And with that, he launched himself from the safety of shadows out into the open. Boldly, he walked past the rundown houses towards the square.

'Stop!' he shouted, waving his arms to attract attention. Then, he slung his bow across his shoulders and, as if he were simply taking a Sunday stroll, sauntered towards the crowd.

The Sheriff and Gisborne watched Robin with surprise that quickly turned to delight.

Robin grinned back at them. 'Good speech, Sheriff,' he said. 'Impressive logic. I wonder – if

I tell you where I am, can *I* claim the twenty pounds? That would be a pound or so for each family here. They could eat a whole winter off that.'

'Amusing,' said the Sheriff with a grim smile. 'Put down your weapon – you are surrounded.'

Eagerly, Gisborne spoke up. 'I am Guy of Gisborne, the new lord of this manor and soon to be Earl of Huntingdon!' he announced. 'Your presence here...' he threw Robin a self-satisfied smile '...is no longer required. Put down your weapon.'

With a cheeky grin, Robin whipped the bow from his shoulders and – *twang!* – fired it at Gisborne. Even though there was no arrow, the new lord of the manor jumped. Realising his mistake, he reddened with fury.

Robin chuckled to himself and obediently placed his bow on the ground. Within seconds, he was surrounded. The cold tips of sharpened broadswords pressed into his throat, while his arms were tightly lashed behind his back.

Meanwhile, the Sheriff nodded to his henchmen, who released Alice and the captive villagers. 'Good,' he said, majestically sweeping his cloak around him and preparing for the journey home. The waiting game was over. Robin of Locksley was his prisoner and he would see to it that, this time, *no one* set him free.

Much and the others watched sadly as Robin was bound for the third time that day.

'I liked him,' said Will. He nodded wistfully.

'I did not,' said Little John.

Outraged beyond belief, Much whirled round to face them both. 'Robin saved your wife!' he cried, before looking over at Will. 'Liked?' he spluttered. 'He's not *dead*.'

The rest of the party lowered their eyes. He might not be dead now. But, at the mercy of the Sheriff of Nottingham, they feared he soon would be.

Kind-hearted Much began to sob. What would he do without his master?

Robin of Locksley stood patiently while the Sheriff and his men readied themselves for departure. His bound wrists were now tied to a long rope that was securely attached to the Sheriff's saddle. It would not be a pleasant journey.

He was right.

Before they moved off, one of the guards struck Robin to the ground. The Sheriff beamed widely as he swept away on horseback, listening to Robin skittering along behind him.

'That was a cruel game to play,' muttered Robin, as the horse slowed to walking pace. Unable to get to his feet, he grimaced as he was forced to crawl behind the trotting hooves.

'Play?' said the Sheriff. His face was mocking. 'You don't understand. You don't play *games* with me. You made a mistake, trying to be the peasants' hero.'

Robin hadn't warmed to the Sheriff much to begin with. And the more he found out about this despicable man, the less he liked him. Why would someone treat his subjects so badly?

41

It defied explanation. Robin could see that the Sheriff like playing mind games and loved a challenge.

'Then why don't *you* be the peasants' hero and show me how it's done?' Robin questioned, daring the Sheriff to show that he was better than Robin, and would do something just to prove his point.

His captor nodded slowly. 'Ah…' he said. 'Do you think we should have a meeting in the morning to discuss it?' A cruel smile began to play at the corners of his mouth. 'A clue: no. You'll *hang* in the morning.' He laughed long and loud.

Now it was clear to Robin that it was pointless appealing to the Sheriff's better nature. He obviously didn't have one.

The Sheriff smiled broadly at the peasants who lined the route as they went past. The villagers stared back, stony-faced, as Robin of Locksley was roughly dragged from the village where he'd grown up.

'Awww…' murmured the Sheriff mockingly.

'All hope lost.'

Much, much later, the Sheriff and his men arrived at the castle. Robin slumped to the ground behind the Sheriff's horse. He was battered, bruised and humiliated beyond belief.

By contrast, Gisborne seemed livelier than ever. With a spring in his step, he leapt down from his saddle.

Robin stared up, his vision blurred by the dirt and sweat of the journey. Clumsily, he tried to brush it away with his cuffs. Now, towering above him, he saw enormous twin gatehouses, guarding the entrance to Nottingham Castle – the Sheriff's home.

Then he saw her, carrying a basket of food. Her long, dark hair tumbled over her shoulders, framing her delicate features. She was wearing a long, pale dress whose hem and cuffs were so long that they brushed the ground. It was Marian. Their eyes met and Robin watched with delight as she stopped dead in her tracks.

So she *did* feel something for him then. He knew it.

Gisborne acknowledged Marian with a jaunty wave, before turning to smile smugly at Robin, as he strode past, towards the main gate. It was hard not be envious. To himself, Robin couldn't deny that he missed Marian. He was led towards the castle, past Marian, the object of his affection, who was still frozen to the spot. She watched as he stumbled by. But she didn't watch with love. Nor even pity. She watched him with disdain.

CHAPTER FIVE

The deer turned slowly above the campfire, its meat crackling and sputtering in the scorching heat. The outlaws were scattered around the fire, making the most of this opportunity to eat so well. Food in the forest was pretty scarce, and it might be days before they ate anything much again. They glanced up disinterestedly when the small party arrived.

Much, Will, Allan, Roy, Forrest and Little John slumped down on the ground, staring listlessly into the flames.

'We rich?' said Hanton, his mouth full of delicious venison.

Little John looked away, visibly upset.

Hanton swallowed what he was eating. 'What's the matter?' he said, before taking another bite.

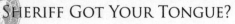

'Saw his wife,' muttered Allan A Dale.

'No reward?' asked Hanton.

'My master gave *himself* in,' said Much crossly. Did these men think of nothing but money?

'To the Sheriff?' said Hanton, who seemed to be having an awful lot of trouble understanding what had gone on. Or perhaps he was just too interested in his dinner.

'The Sheriff was cutting out tongues!' said Much. 'He could hardly stand by and watch people lose their tongues.'

'Hey,' Hanton said, as if a wonderful idea had just occurred to him. 'That would be funny, wouldn't it? If, instead of "cat got your tongue?" they said, "Sheriff got your tongue?"'

'What?' said Much, not entirely sure he'd heard correctly.

'If someone was, you know, a bit quiet,' said Hanton, 'you'd go, "What's the matter? Sheriff got your tongue?"'

Much shook his head in exasperation. 'You can't just sit there,' he said to Hanton and the assembled outlaws. 'We've got to do something.

We've got to go to Nottingham and… and… get him out,' he finished lamely.

'How?' asked Will. It was difficult enough getting into Nottingham Castle, never mind getting out again. He ought to know. Quickly, he thought back to the previous day, when he'd stood at the castle with a noose around his neck – ready to be hanged. He shuddered.

'No point anyway,' grumbled Allan.

Now Much was becoming really angry. 'No point?' he shouted. 'You would be dead if Robin had not…' His words petered out as he too remembered the daring rescue. 'You would be dead.'

'True,' said Allan. 'Mind you, I wasn't supposed to hang in the first place. That was just a confusion.'

'We cannot let him die,' Much whispered. He turned to his friend for support. 'Will?'

But Will could only shrug helplessly. And as far as he could see, it was Robin's bravery that had saved him and the others the day before. And if Robin wasn't here to help them, how could they hope to succeed now?

'Very well.' Instantly, Much's mind was made up. 'I shall go alone.'

'See you!' Cheerily, Roy waved goodbye.

Filled with purpose, Much went towards Robin's horse. But Roy shook his head. Great. It looked like he'd be walking then. With his shoulders back and his head held high, Much marched bravely into the thick, green foliage. No one attempted to stop him. But no one joined him either.

'Everyone!' cried Hanton excitedly. While they'd all been talking about Robin, the outlaw had been loitering around the roasting deer. 'Look!' he said, prising open the deer's mouth. There was no tongue inside. 'What's the matter, deer?' he asked, suppressing a giggle. 'Sheriff got your tongue?' And, with a flourish, he produced the missing tongue from behind his back, waving it to and fro before the outlaws.

Nobody laughed. Little John fired a particularly disapproving look in Hanton's direction.

'What?' grumbled the outlaw, throwing the

tongue on the fire. It sizzled loudly before shrivelling into a charred lump. 'How come no one can take a joke all of a sudden?' He trudged back to where he'd left his meal and carried on eating.

For a few moments, no one spoke. Then Little John stood up and marched purposefully towards Will. 'In which house is my wife?' he demanded. 'I am going to fetch her.'

'Fetch her where?' asked Will.

'Here,' said John. 'A woman can live here, same as us.'

Will shook his head. 'Alice can't live in the forest,' he said.

'Why not?'

'Ah…' It all became clear. Will suddenly realised that Little John didn't know. He didn't have a clue why his poor, abandoned wife couldn't live in the forest with them all.

It was about time he found out.

The dungeons were hewn out of rock, deep below Nottingham Castle. They were cold, damp, very dark and exceedingly smelly. By now, Robin had grown used to the sound of rats' claws, as they scampered here and there, scrabbling for morsels of food. And it didn't look as if he'd be here too long, not if they were going to hang him in the morning. He gave the chains that held him a tug, but they held firm. No chance of escape then.

The jailer shuffled towards him. 'Not so high and mighty now, are we?' he jeered, his mouth so close that Robin could feel tiny droplets of spit landing on his face.

It wasn't worth answering.

Without warning, the jailer's fist darted out and slammed into Robin's stomach. He doubled up in agony, aware that the assistant jailer was guffawing loudly.

'That's for the priest trick,' snarled the jailer. He spoke of the man who had posed as a holy man the day before. The plan was to prevent Will and the others from hanging on the grounds that they'd enrolled in the church. Unfortunately, it had failed.

'Could have cost me my job,' he added bitterly.

Robin was unrepentant. 'One job to save four lives,' was his reasoning.

The jailer threatened to punch Robin again, but he pulled away at the last moment. Angrily, he undid Robin's chains and dragged him roughly along a dank corridor. The dungeons they passed were overflowing with miserable inmates.

'He won't be saving you now, my lovelies, wherever you're from,' the jailer crowed at the curious prisoners. 'He's not Robin of Locksley any more!'

'Robin Wood, they're calling him,' muttered his assistant, as they entered a cramped cell, designed for one.

The jailer misheard. 'Robin Hood?' he said, addressing his prisoner with glee. 'There'll be no hood tomorrow morning. Sheriff wants the rabble to see the fear in your eyes. Wants 'em to see your eyes pop right out!' He looked at Robin and cackled loudly.

And with that parting shot, he and his assistant left, leaving Robin alone to contemplate his fate.

Tomorrow, he would die.

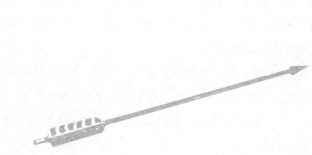

CHAPTER SIX

B y sunset, Much was weary of travelling. He'd avoided the paths and tracks that led through Sherwood Forest – he couldn't risk capture again – and had ploughed his way through the dense undergrowth instead. He'd long since grown tired of dodging the low branches and thorny bushes that blocked his way. Now, he just wanted to reach his journey's end.

It was with a huge sigh of relief that he saw Knighton Hall, and with rather less excitement that he saw the two spies loitering outside. Hastily, he ducked behind an outbuilding to escape their watchful eyes. The two men strolled back and forth, eventually turning away from Much. He took his chance, creeping towards the main house, step by step by…

Wallop! Down he went, like a sack of potatoes. With a muffled cry, Much clutched his ankle. He'd twisted it as he fell and it was pure agony. Almost sobbing with the pain, Much scrambled to his feet and limped towards the back door. It was Marian who opened it.

'Quickly, your ladyship,' said Much. 'My master is arrested. He has been taken to Nottingham.'

'I know.' Marian spoke calmly. Her beautiful face gave away not even a flicker of emotion. 'You cannot be here.'

'It is safe,' said Much. 'I have not been seen.' Then he suddenly realised what she'd said. 'You *know*?'

Marian looked nervously to the left and right, checking that they were not watched. When she was sure the coast was clear, she dragged Much inside.

'Nothing?' asked Much incredulously. This was not something he had anticipated, not from Edward, the kind retired Sheriff and a man who knew the difference between right and wrong. He had never been like this before he and Robin went on the crusades.

But Edward had changed. Instead of the sprightly man of old, he now seemed shrunken, a mere shadow of his former self. His clear, confident gaze was gone – he watched Much with unease bordering on fear. 'What can *I* do?' he said. 'I warned him. This Sheriff…' His voice trailed away.

'Yes, my lord,' said Much. 'But – '

'He should have listened to my father,' interrupted Marian, her voice cold. 'Now he is an outlaw.'

'I know, your ladyship, but – '

'And not a very impressive one,' she added.

'That is not – forgive me – that is not fair,' Much said passionately. 'He is *most* impressive.'

'He is caught,' stated Marian. 'And after just one day. Does that impress you?'

Much squared his shoulders and stared right into the watery depths of Marian's blue eyes. 'He gave himself up to save tongues,' he said simply.

This was news to Marian and she flinched nervously. 'Tongues?'

'In Locksley,' explained Much. 'The Sheriff was cutting out people's tongues... until somebody told him where Robin was.' Anger transformed his kindly face. 'I hate the Sheriff,' he said, the words laced with venom. He focussed his angry gaze on the old Sheriff and his daughter. 'And I hate *you* if you aren't going to help Robin.'

In the stunned silence that followed, Much spun on his heel and marched – or would have marched if his injured ankle hadn't been aching so furiously – towards the door.

'Young man!' Edward sounded genuinely upset. 'I will speak in court, of course, but... your master has doomed himself. His fate is...' Here, his words petered out and he shrugged helplessly. 'Resign yourself,' he said.

Much turned to Marian. 'In the Holy Land, my master had dreams,' he whispered. 'He spoke your name.'

Visibly shaken by this unexpected news, the

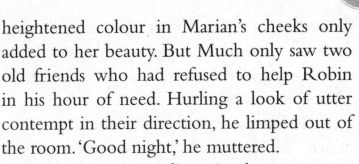

heightened colour in Marian's cheeks only added to her beauty. But Much only saw two old friends who had refused to help Robin in his hour of need. Hurling a look of utter contempt in their direction, he limped out of the room. 'Good night,' he muttered.

There was no point lingering here.

Little John watched the tattered, run-down house from the cover of nearby trees. He'd been there for hours, waiting for the tiniest glimpse. At last, he got it. A small, fragile-looking boy limped out of the house. Little John stifled a gasp. Then, checking that the coast was clear, he broke cover.

'Psst!' he called.

The child turned. 'Who are you?' he asked curiously.

'Who are *you*?' asked Little John. He had to make sure.

'John,' replied the boy.

'John what?'

'John Little.'

'Oh,' said Little John quietly. Inside, he was elated. So it *was* true! A feeling of indescribable happiness surged through him as he looked at his son.

'But everyone calls me Little John,' the child added. 'You know why?' He smiled broadly, as if he had the best secret ever.

'Why?' Little John could hardly bear to hear the answer.

'Because my father was called John too,' explained the boy. 'John Little. He was a hero. He was big, I think.' At this, he looked vaguely confused, but shrugged and continued. 'People called him Little John too. What is *your* name?'

Little John wanted so desperately to reveal his name that it hurt. But he couldn't – not when staying silent was the only way of protecting his boy. 'I am a friend of your mother's,' he said instead. 'How is she?'

The child rolled his eyes. 'She is always tired, always sewing,' he grumbled. 'But do you know what?'

'What?' asked Little John.

'Everything is going to be good now Robin is back from the Holy Land.' The little boy looked very excited by this announcement.

'Oh.' The words stung. A feeling of hot shame began to invade Little John's thoughts, no matter how much he pushed it away.

But there was more. 'He always makes sure everyone has enough to eat,' said the child proudly. '*We* had a feast at the big house. *I* had so much pork my belly ached! Mother had fish, but…' He screwed up his face. 'Fish, I do not like.'

By now, Little John didn't know whether to laugh or cry. 'Fish is her favourite,' he said simply.

The boy stared innocently into Little John's eyes. 'Robin *will* come back from Nottingham, won't he?' he asked.

'I…'

Luckily for Little John, he was saved from replying by a familiar voice. 'Little John?' cried Alice. 'Where are you, Little John?'

'That's Mother,' said the child. 'Do you want

to come in?'

He gave a sad smile. 'I don't think I can come in, Little John,' he said tenderly. Too much time had passed. Alice had learned to live without him. And – worst of all – he was an outlaw. If anyone discovered that he wasn't a dead man, then Alice's life would be in danger – and his son's life too.

Alice peered out of the door, smiling as she saw her tiny son. He grinned back, and then turned to his new friend to introduce him. But Little John had vanished.

'It is late,' said Alice softly. 'Come on.' She scooped him up into her arms and began to make her way back to the house. She paused once, glancing over her shoulder to the dark, rustling leaves of Sherwood Forest as if sensing a familiar presence. Then she shook her head, to dislodge the feeling, and disappeared inside.

Later that evening, when the first stars were twinkling in a clear sky, Alice put her son to bed. It was a rickety cot – a hand-me-down from another kindly villager – but it was comfortable enough. She smoothed a piece of sacking over the child and tucked him in securely. Then crouching beside him, she began to sing a lullaby. It wasn't very good – she'd thought up the words and the tune herself – but Little John loved it.

Have you ever kissed a boy called John?
For if you've never kissed a boy called John
You don't know what you've missed
Not kissing Little John.
Not kissing Little John.

Not two feet away from Alice and her son sat Little John, leaning against the flimsy wall of the house. As he listened to the lullaby, his eyes filled with tears. She hadn't forgotten him.

In that moment, Little John made a life-changing decision. He pulled himself to his feet and took a deep breath: time to stop being dead.

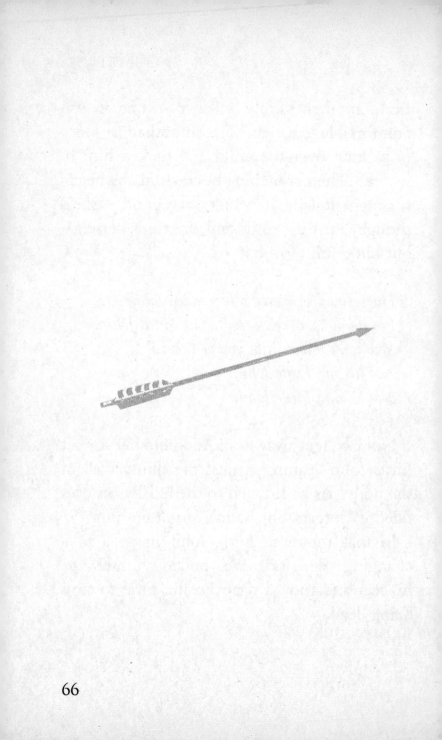

CHAPTER SEVEN

It was long after nightfall when Much reached Nottingham Castle. He was tired, he was hungry and his ankle hurt so badly that it felt as if it were on fire. When he saw the armed guards at the castle entrance, his heart dropped. His brave plan of action had extended as far as the castle – but no further. He'd simply assumed that he would get in. He hadn't worked out how.

There was a loud *thunk*. Much looked round to see two hefty delivery men unloading wooden barrels from a cart nearby. They each shouldered a barrel and headed towards the castle entrance and what lay beyond. Instantly, Much's spirits lifted. Perhaps there was a way in after all…

With as much nonchalance as he could muster,

he made his way over to the cart. Selecting a barrel, he hoisted it quickly onto his shoulder. *Whoa!* He hadn't guessed quite how heavy it would be. Nevertheless, bracing himself and ignoring the pain in his ankle, Much hurried after the delivery men. They hadn't got far – the two men had only reached the castle entrance, where they were waiting to be admitted.

The castle guard nodded curtly, signalling that the men could go through. Hastily, Much followed, hardly able to believe his good luck.

'Oi, you!' Filled with foreboding, Much stopped. 'No.' He turned with dismay to see that it was the guard who had spoken. He was pointing right at Robin's would-be saviour.

'Get lost, turd face,' said the guard.

Much dropped the barrel with a resounding clang and scampered away. He was ashamed of himself. He'd flattered himself that he could complete a daring rescue alone, but he couldn't even get into Nottingham Castle.

His master was doomed.

Meanwhile, inside the castle dungeons, it was visiting hours.

Robin listened as the heavy door leading to the dungeons was unlocked and the sound of many footsteps barged along the corridor towards his cell. With a great rattling of keys, the jailer unlocked the cell gate and his visitor appeared. It was, of course, the Sheriff of Nottingham. The man was taking no chances – four burly guards who crowded inside the cell doorway, ready to leap to his defence at a moment's notice, accompanied him. The jailer locked the door with an ominous click.

The Sheriff stared at Robin, his beady eyes glinting in the half-light. 'I've realised something about you,' he said.

'I thought you didn't want to talk,' Robin muttered.

'That was before I realised.'

'Realised what?'

The Sheriff took a deep breath. 'You're a renowned marksman with the bow,' he began. 'You saw me, ready to excise a tongue or two.

You could have shot me.'

Robin was silent.

'Why didn't you?' asked the Sheriff.

'You had men everywhere,' replied his prisoner. 'I had only a few. We were outnumbered.' As he spoke, his face displayed no emotion.

'Oh, yes,' said the Sheriff briskly. 'I'm sure all that's true. But you gave yourself up…' He looked genuinely puzzled.

For what it was worth, Robin decided to tell the truth. 'I care about those people – my people,' he said. 'More than I care about myself. You would not understand.'

'Oh, yeah, yeah, yeah…' The Sheriff of Nottingham brushed away this answer as if it meant nothing at all. 'But that's not the point. Do you want to know what the point is?'

'No.'

The Sheriff continued regardless. 'The point is: you care more about *my* life than you do about yours.' He looked delighted with his own insight.

'No.'

'Then why didn't you kill me? You must have known I would see you executed.'

Robin looked away, troubled by these words. Could it be that the Sheriff spoke the truth? Or was he simply twisting the facts to unsettle him? He felt suddenly afraid of his own feelings.

'Lost your nerve?' probed his inquisitor. 'Lost your taste for blood? Robin of Locksley, honoured for his service in the King's private guard… How many must you have killed in the Holy Land? And yet here we are in Locksley, where people who love you best of all are in danger. You have the chance to shoot. And you don't take it.'

'I would kill you in an instant!' spat Robin.

The Sheriff smiled. 'Maybe,' he said, 'if it was the only way to prevent bloodshed. But it wasn't the only way, was it? You didn't have to kill me, because you could sacrifice yourself. And that's what you did.'

'Think of me what you will,' said Robin in a low voice. 'If I am to hang in the morning, it makes no difference.' He turned away. He must not let this man's evil words seep into his mind. He must *not*.

'Ahhh…' sighed the Sheriff. 'He doesn't want to talk. Jailer,' he commanded. 'Open the gate.'

The gate creaked open.

'You are free to go,' said the Sheriff.

Hardly able to believe what he was hearing or seeing, Robin stared at the open doorway.

'But then if you go,' added his captor, 'you may find tomorrow that one or two of your villagers won't be on, shall we say, "speaking terms" with you.' His mouth twisted into an evil smile.

And there was the final blow. He could leave – but only at the expense of more tongues. It was despicable. Robin narrowed his eyes and poured all of the hatred he felt into his gaze.

'I like this,' said the Sheriff, delighted at his idea and at Robin's response. 'This is good. I may give the jailer the night off, and leave your cell open… Just for the fun of knowing you are trapped by your own cowardice.' He beamed, getting into his stride now. 'Yes, and tomorrow,

I could give the executioner the day off and have you hang *yourself* for my sport. Do you tie a good noose, Huntingdon?'

Robin's words were filled with loathing. 'I do not know why Englishmen travel two thousand miles to fight evil, when the real cancer is here,' he said bitterly.

'I can hear a noise,' said the Sheriff, cupping a hand to his ear and addressing the others. 'Can you hear a noise?' He paused theatrically. 'I think it's a dead man talking,' he said. And with that, he whirled round and stalked out of the cell, followed by his guards.

The jailer locked the gate, watching Robin curiously through the bars. 'I'd have gone, if I was you,' he said.

In reply, Robin leapt into the air and grasped a sturdy wooden beam. He hung there motionless before beginning a series of punishing chin-ups. He needed to be at his peak for the hours ahead. It might make all the difference. 'You're not me,' he said grimly.

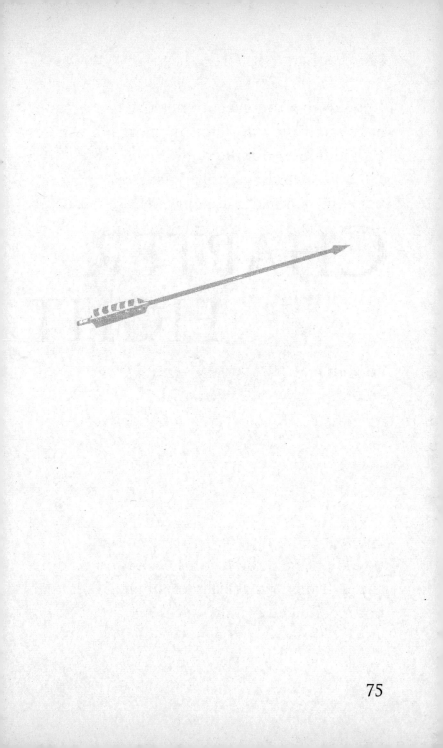

CHAPTER EIGHT

Deep in Sherwood Forest, the motley group of men sat around the dying embers of the campfire, staring fixedly into the rippling glow.

'Think the whiney one will make it?' said Forrest thoughtfully.

'What's he going to do?' asked Roy. 'Stroll into Nottingham and say, "Excuse me, can my friend Lavender Boy go free?"'

The outlaws laughed uproariously, but not Will and Allan A Dale. Will especially looked furious.

'Lambs to the slaughter, both of them,' said Roy. His voice was less jovial now, as if he were only now imagining what Robin and Much must be going through.

'Could have given him the horse…' said

Allan quietly.

'Then we lose a horse too,' said Forrest, with a shrug. 'Think about it.'

The selfish comment tipped Will over the edge. 'If Robin dies, the people of Locksley will be like you!' he cried.

'What do you mean, like us?' asked Forrest. He wore a look of total bewilderment.

'They will have nothing left to live for,' Will explained. 'They will be dead men…' He flinched as Roy grabbed him angrily.

'*You* go and save him then,' Roy threatened. 'See you!' Roy twisted his hand tighter in the fabric at Will's neck, making him choke. 'We don't do town,' he growled. 'We're outlaws. We're on the run.'

'And what will happen to the loved ones you leave behind?' squeaked Will, wriggling his neck in an attempt to get more air.

'Town is death,' said Roy ominously.

Will tried just one more time. 'Have you seen what happens to a family when there is only one breadwinner?' he said.

'Heartbreaking.' Without warning, Roy let go of his victim, letting him crash to the ground. 'Are you deaf?' he growled. 'We don't go to Nottingham.'

At the sound of footsteps, everyone looked up. It was Little John, returned from his visit to Locksley. He towered before them, wearing an expression of grim intent. 'We go to Nottingham,' he announced.

Marian had company. Apprehensively, she glanced at the unwelcome guest, whose eyes were fixed on the servant as he poured wine. He accepted a goblet and, from his trembling hand, it appeared that he too was nervous.

'I would be pleased if you would come and visit me in Locksley,' said Guy of Gisborne. 'Now that it is mine.'

Desperately, Marian wracked her brains for an excuse. Gisborne was nothing if not persistent in his demands to see her. There was no doubting that he was a handsome man, but something about him disturbed Marian. But, in times like these, it was dangerous to offend such an important man. 'I… do not know,' she said eventually.

Gisborne rambled on regardless. 'It is a fair place,' he said. 'Modest. I have ambitions that are greater, of course. You know that. But for now, to have land once more in the Gisborne name…' He paused and his cruel eyes softened. 'My father would be proud.'

'I am glad for you,' said Marian, through gritted teeth.

Her guest spoke slowly, as if the words hurt him. 'Some of my men – I know this for a fact – used to laugh at my title. Guy of Gisborne has little meaning when there *is* no Gisborne.'

Was she supposed to feel sorry for him, this man who had wreaked havoc in Locksley and now hoped to steal another man's land, his village and his people? 'And Locksley is your Gisborne?' she whispered.

'Yes, actually,' Gisborne replied. He seemed pleased, proud almost. 'I am intent on changing its name.'

This was too much. 'Does changing a name really make a difference?' asked Marian. Faced with this callous behaviour, she was having the greatest difficulty hiding her dislike.

'When a woman marries,' Gisborne said softly, 'she changes her name. It makes a difference.' His gaze was intense and filled with unmistakeable meaning.

Hastily, Marian tried to change the subject. 'What of Robin?' she asked.

'What *of* Robin?'

'He will contest your acquisition of his lands, surely.'

'He will die.'

Even though he spoke of the man who had abandoned her to follow the King, leaving her heartbroken, Marian still felt sickened by his attitude. Robin deserved justice, the same as any other. '*If* he is found guilty,' she insisted.

'There is no need for a trial.' Gisborne seemed quite certain of this. 'He will hang in the morning.'

Something was wrong here. *Very* wrong.

'There must be a trial,' said Marian, growing nervous now. 'It is the law.'

'But he is an outlaw,' said Gisborne. 'The Sheriff, in these straitened times, has made special provision. Outlaws are classed as enemies of war. Thus, we can hold them without trial.' He smiled, before delivering the final blow. 'We can *execute* without trial.'

'No!' Marian gasped, unable to believe what she had just heard. 'It… it cannot be.'

'We are at war,' Gisborne stated baldly.

'We are at war *in the Holy Land*,' said Marian. 'It does not mean we dispense with justice here.'

Her father hurried into the room.

'I am so sorry to keep you waiting.' Edward was apologetic. 'I was not expecting you.'

When Marian spoke, her voice was icy. 'Do not worry, Father,' she said. 'Sir Guy was just leaving.'

Not a million miles away, Much loitered around the outer walls of Nottingham Castle, looking for a way in. When he spotted a ladder half-hidden in the undergrowth, he almost whooped with happiness – and would have done if there weren't guards nearby. His daring rescue was back on track!

First checking that no one watched him, Much propped the old, wooden ladder up against the rough stone wall. Eagerly, he scrambled up and up and... no further.

The ladder was too short.

Much stared at the top of the wall, which was so close, but just out of reach. He felt like crying. Utterly defeated, he started to descend. Then he froze in horror as a deep, vicious growl rumbled beneath him. He looked down. And there, at the foot of the ladder, was a fierce guard dog. It snarled again. Even from this great height, Much could see its teeth.

'Go away,' said Much. 'Shoo. Shoo!'

His words made no difference whatsoever – the dog wasn't going anywhere.

Much was trapped.

Six hours later, as dawn began to break, Much was still trapped. He clung to the ladder, his fingers grown numb with cold, his face rigid with fear. He was exhausted beyond belief, so tired that he felt sure he would tumble to his death before very much longer. And who would help Robin then?

Much heard footsteps. They were coming towards him, moving closer and closer. Panic gripped him. He was about to be captured! He closed his eyes in terrified anticipation, expecting the worst…

'Who's a good boy, eh?'

That didn't sound like a murderous guard. Cautiously, Much opened his eyes and peered downwards. There, far below, was Allan A Dale! He was petting the vicious guard dog, which had miraculously transformed into a loveable puppy. Astonished, Much watched as the dog began to lick his friend's hand.

'Need any help?' called Allan.

Much nodded speechlessly, beginning his descent of the ladder. Then his eyes grew wider than ever as he saw Will, Little John, Roy and Forrest emerge from the shadowy trees. He was stunned. They'd come to find him? They'd come to help him rescue Robin? Quickly, he tried to change his terrified expression to a braver, bolder one. He didn't want them to think he'd been scared.

'I was just… er… checking up there for a moment,' he blustered. 'And, as I suspected, the ladder is useless.' He hopped from the last rung to the soft, springy ground.

Little John nodded at Roy.

'Right you are,' replied the outlaw. He hefted the ladder into the air and helped Little John to balance it on his shoulders, holding it steady as they slowly leaned it towards the wall.

Much squinted upwards, grinning with delight as he saw that the highest rung of the ladder was now level with the top of the castle wall. With a curt nod, Little John signalled to Much to climb the ladder once more.

They were going in.

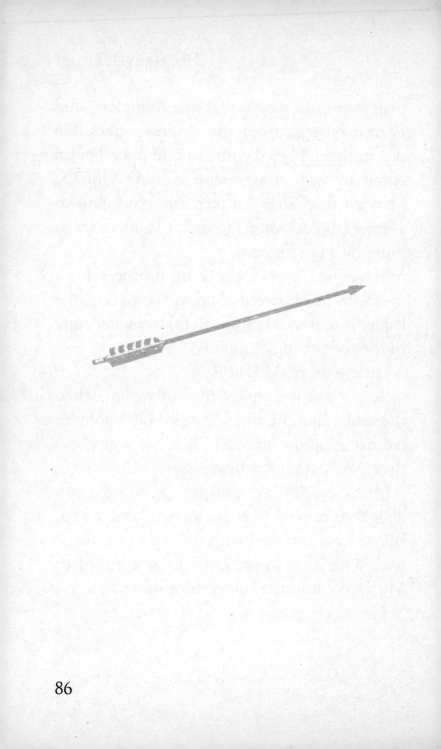

CHAPTER NINE

Daylight had no chance of reaching the gloomy dungeons, so Robin sensed rather than knew that it was morning. He paced to and fro in his tiny cell, his mind racing. Time was short – how could he get out of this fix?

He heard footsteps, more than one set. They progressed along the corridor and as they passed the cell gate, Robin glimpsed the one person he never thought he would see here. Marian. She scowled at him, before following the jailer out of sight. Robin frowned – now he was confused.

After a moment, the jailer reappeared. He studied his prisoner with a mischievous glint in his eye, jangling his keys before he inserted one in the lock. It turned smoothly. 'Come on, then,' he said. 'Let's have some entertainment, my lovely.'

The jailer opened the gate and led the way into another cell – this one with furniture. Inside, stood Marian. She was still scowling. Robin was beginning to think scowling was all she ever did nowadays. He remembered when she used to smile…

'Where is it?' she asked, neatly interrupting his thoughts.

This wasn't quite what Robin had expected. 'Where is what?'

'Please.' Marian's tone was sarcastic in the extreme. 'The ring my father gave you years ago,' she went on, 'before he knew the wickedness of your heart.'

'I…' Robin didn't have a clue what she was talking about. Had he missed something?

The jailer spoke up. 'I told you, madam. Asking doesn't usually work. I'll do his thumbs,' he added helpfully, unhooking a set of vicious-looking thumbscrews from the wall.

Marian looked suspicious. 'Will these work?' she asked.

'These?' The jailer regarded the torture device with pride. 'They're lovely.'

'When he talks, you will hear?' she asked.

'Well, yes…' replied the jailor cautiously.

'That I cannot allow,' said Marian firmly. 'You might get there first and steal the ring.'

'Madam, I assure you,' said the jailer, 'I am a man of small pleasures. Inflicting pain, that is enough for mc.'

'Maybe,' said Marian. 'But if the ring is not where he tells me, suspicion will fall on you… and that would be unfair.' She breathed in deeply, assuming an air of great authority. 'I will try speaking with him first. You may go.'

'I can't do that,' said the jailer.

'Wait outside.' Marian waved an arm imperiously in the direction of the doorway. 'He cannot escape and he will not dare to attack me.'

'No, I…'

'Leave.'

'Yes, your ladyship.' Looking exceedingly disgruntled, the jailer left the room, locking the door behind him.

Marian turned to Robin and coolly he met her gaze, aware that he was in for a tongue-lashing. Marian had never been one to mince her words.

'You are an utter fool,' she spat.

'You said that already,' said Robin, thinking back to the tirade of words she'd unleashed on him a few days earlier.

'Oh, you listened?' she said angrily. 'I also told you that confronting the Sheriff would not work. You didn't listen to *that*.'

Robin shrugged. 'I did not have much choice,' he said.

Marian's eyes bored into his. 'Everything is a choice. Everything we do,' she said. 'Grow up.'

This stung. 'I prevented unjust hangings,' protested Robin. 'I protected people from my village…'

'That would make your death…' Marian paused, as if thinking of exactly the right word. 'Romantic,' she concluded.

Robin disagreed with this wholeheartedly. 'It

would make it *honourable.*'

Marian tutted. But she wasn't finished, not by any means. 'And the people you were so honourably protecting? Who will protect them when you are dead?' She paused, allowing her words time to hit their mark before attacking from another angle. 'What is it with men and glory? Glory above sense, above reason…?'

'It is principle,' said Robin. He knew her words made sense, but he couldn't help the way he felt, the way he acted.

Marian hit back at once. 'Principle is making a difference,' she snapped. 'And that is hard when you're dead. You could have stayed here in the first place, instead of following the King to the Holy Land, if you had wanted to look after your precious people. But you didn't.' Her eyes were filled with contempt. 'You chose war. You chose glory.' She was flushed with anger – and with another less obvious emotion too. What could it be?

'What is this about?' Robin's voice was soft, cajoling and suddenly, Marian seemed terribly vulnerable.

'It's about you saying you care about… the people of Locksley,' she said hesitantly, as if she were talking not about the villagers, but another person altogether. Herself. 'When the truth is you ran off to battle thousands of miles away.'

Robin reached forward and stroked her face gently. She flinched from his touch and glared angrily at him. 'You had something on your cheek,' he lied.

'Right!' Marian was at once brisk and businesslike. 'This is what we do. Stand by the door. I will scream. In he comes. You strike him and run. I have paid a man at the East Gate – you will not be seen if you go now, before the day watch.' From inside her cloak, she produced a dagger and a set of keys. 'Take these.'

'I cannot go unseen,' said Robin calmly.

'You cannot go seen!'

'I cannot let the Sheriff win.'

It was a battle of wills.

'You have not heard a single word I said, have you?' Marian stormed.

'Trust me,' he said. 'I have a plan... well, half a plan.' Robin's eyes flashed with excitement, as silently, he implored her to understand.

Instead, she was livid.

'I love it when you look at me in anger,' whispered Robin.

Marian groaned loudly with frustration as her carefully laid plan crumbled to dust. But now she'd alerted the jailer. He started to fumble with the door lock – any second now, he would be inside the room. Quickly, Robin skipped behind the door and raised his fist, ready to knock the jailer to the ground.

The door swung open. The jailer looked at Marian oddly before crashing forward onto the stone floor. As he fell, a terrified-looking Much was revealed, wielding a large lump of wood. Behind him stood Will and Allan A Dale, watching with astonishment and then joy as the jailer collapsed.

'This is a rescue!' announced Much unnecessarily.

Robin poked his head around the door and

grinned widely at his men. He deftly caught the bow and quiver of arrows that they threw to him.

'And we are undetected!' added Much.

He spoke too soon. Distant shouting and a tremendous banging interrupted the reunion – it sounded as if guards were at the main entrance to the dungeons.

'Ah,' said Much.

Finally, the dungeon door gave way, crashing to the ground with an almighty clang. Six burly guards stormed through the doorway, thundering down the corridor. But it was empty – there was no sign of any outlaws. The prisoners watched in dumb amazement from their cells. It was the most exciting thing that had happened in weeks.

'Help!' cried Marian.

Instantly, the guards pounded in the direction of her voice.

Quietly, taking great care not to rattle them, Robin took the jailer's keys from his pocket.

He opened the cell gate and – one by one – he, Much, Will and Allan crept into the corridor, before heading for the dungeon entrance and freedom.

Expecting to find Marian held at arrow-point by the outlaw, Robin Hood, the guards were somewhat bemused to find her sitting on the stone floor, where she cradled the unconscious jailer's head in her lap.

'Thank God,' said Marian, wide-eyed with innocence. 'This man needs help.'

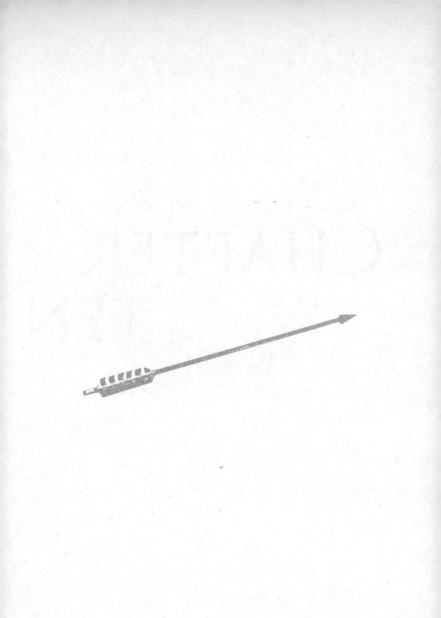

CHAPTER TEN

Robin and his three rescuers burst out of a side door into the courtyard of Nottingham Castle. At once, Little John and the outlaws stepped out of the shadows, where they had waited to avoid detection – they looked mightily relieved to see that the small party was safe.

'Thank you for coming,' said Robin gratefully to Little John.

The big man nodded solemnly.

'Let's go before they see we've opened the gates,' Roy urged. He looked eager to be gone.

Robin glanced towards the courtyard entrance. The gates were indeed ajar. Through the tiny gap, freedom beckoned irresistibly. But he shook his head. There was something he needed to do first. 'Hold an escape route for me. I need five minutes,' said Robin. 'If I am longer than that, leave without me.'

All eyes were on Little John, as if he were the only one qualified to make such a decision. He hesitated… then nodded.

'Thank you,' said Robin again. He shielded his eyes from the unaccustomed brightness of the daylight and scanned the battlements, working out his plan.

Much looked very worried indeed. 'Master, no!' he implored. 'You cannot go back in. If you go back in and die, *I* will die – of grief. So you must come with us, if only to save me.'

Robin chuckled. 'That is why I love you,' he said fondly. 'And…' his eyes roamed the group of outlaws, landing on Roy '…you. Can you help me?' His expression was serious. 'It is dangerous.'

Caught off guard, Roy hesitated. But Little John threw him a stern look and he agreed. 'Yes.'

'Why him, if you love me?' complained

Much. 'Why not me?'

He spoke to empty air. Robin had gone, taking Roy with him.

The Sheriff's men charged out of the dungeons in search of the escaped prisoner. But a small band of outlaws lay in wait. Little John and the others set to at once, attacking them with zeal and winning their leader precious seconds.

Clang! Clang! Clang! In the distance, a bell began to chime frantically – the alarm had been raised. Any moment now, the castle would be swarming with guards.

Meanwhile, taking care to remain out of sight, Robin and Roy ran towards a heap of building materials. Robin rummaged among the bricks, planks and tools until he found what he was looking for – a length of rope. His fingers a blur, he tied the rope to the end of an arrow and fired it up, up, up to the grisly gibbet set high on the battlements – the scene of many hangings.

As the last of the Sheriff's men emerged from

the castle, Robin ducked out of sight, pulling Roy with him. They flattened themselves against the wall, breathing heavily until the danger was past. Then the two men dived through the doorway, into the castle itself. Creeping slowly, quietly, along a stone corridor, they saw a guard fumbling with his boots. Nearby hung an array of uniforms, hung neatly on pegs – ready for the taking.

It was almost too easy. One whack from Roy's fist and the man went down. Robin held up a uniform and winked at Roy.

Minutes later, there were two more castle guards. But they didn't follow the orders of the Sheriff. And they certainly weren't hunting for Robin Hood.

The Sheriff of Nottingham stirred. Outside his chamber, he heard the most terrible commotion, followed by a furious pounding on his door.

'My lord!' cried a muffled voice. 'Robin has escaped!'

The Sheriff stumbled, bleary-eyed, towards the door and dragged back the lock. He jumped back in surprise as his sentries tumbled to the ground before him. They were out cold.

In the doorway stood a castle guard, grinning from ear to ear. The Sheriff blinked. Castle guard? No… this was Robin Hood! The outlaw entered the chamber. Behind him lay the slumped bodies of three sentries.

Robin advanced.

The Sheriff backed away fearfully. 'What do you want?' he whined.

'Yesterday, in Locksley, you revealed your true colours,' said Robin. 'Today, I reveal mine.' Casually, he plucked an arrow from his quiver. He'd had ample time in the castle dungeons to prepare his speech. And now the Sheriff was going to hear it. 'You guessed right. I have lost my taste for bloodshed,' he said. His voice hardened. 'But if you *ever* callously, needlessly hurt *anyone* as a way of getting to me… if you cut out a tongue or brand an arm or so much as pluck the hair of an innocent person to get to me… in the name of King Richard, so help me, I will kill *you*.'

By now, the Sheriff had retreated so far that he'd butted up against his ornate, throne-like chair and could go no further. Terrified, but trying desperately not to show it, he sat down abruptly and stared at Robin. The outlaw stared back.

'I don't believe you,' said the Sheriff. Although he spoke bravely, his lip trembled.

'Trust me.' Robin was deadly serious.

'What has changed since yesterday?' the Sheriff spluttered. 'Nothing.'

Wordlessly, Robin placed an arrow against the string of his bow and fired. *Twang!* It hit the chair, landing a short distance away from his captive's hand.

'Prove it,' hissed the Sheriff. 'I will not change, I will stoop low… so kill me now!'

Furiously, Robin fired three arrows in quick succession. They landed with exact precision between the fingers of the Sheriff's left hand, burrowing deep into the mahogany arm of the ornate chair.

'Impressive,' drawled the Sheriff. 'But each arrow fired into the *chair* is a point lost, isn't it?'

Robin said nothing.

The Sheriff of Nottingham rose from his chair, advancing towards Robin. And although Robin drew another arrow from his quiver, the Sheriff was totally confident that he had no desire to fire it. So the Sheriff continued to taunt him. 'What's surprising is that you do not even maim me,' he said. 'I am not even grazed. Surely I deserve that? A minor wound. Then I might take a fever and die, and you could tell yourself it was not your fault.' He put his head on one side and regarded Robin with raised eyebrows. 'But no… not even that. Are you afraid of authority? Or is it secretly that you know I am right and that we must have law and order?' He smiled. 'I think it is. I think that's why I *will* have you hang yourself.'

With a fury he had not known he possessed, Robin dragged the sharp point of the arrow across the back of the Sheriff's hand. It was a deep wound that dripped freely with blood. 'I have maimed you,' he said, feeling no pleasure at the words.

His victim smiled, even though he was obviously in pain. 'A scratch,' he said. 'My point stands.'

Robin took a deep breath. 'Lavender,' he said clearly.

'Lavender?' The Sheriff was confused. 'Hmm. Maybe. But my pain will be salved by a sweeter balm – the knowledge that you are weak…' With every word he grew bolder, because he had seen what Robin could not. One of his fallen sentries had stirred and was now struggling woozily to his feet. 'You are as weak as your charming, *sweet* conscience is strong,' he continued, his eyes flickering towards the sentry as he drew his sword and advanced on Robin.

But Robin had seen the movement of his eyes and – in one deft, shocking movement – he swivelled and fired his arrow, shooting the sentry square in the chest at close range. The man stood no chance and crumpled to the ground. He was dead. Immediately, Robin reloaded his weapon with a fresh arrow and swung back to face the open-mouthed Sheriff. He had clearly not expected this.

'You overestimate my conscience,' muttered Robin, with a grim smile. Menacingly, he moved towards the terrified man, grabbing the leather purse – the very same purse the Sheriff had offered the villagers as a reward – from a nearby table and neatly pocketing it. 'Now,' he said. 'Do precisely as I say.'

'Stop!'
The castle guards looked up from the courtyard – where they were doing their level best to clobber the outlaws – in total confusion. What on earth was their master playing at? One minute they were told to kill anything that moved. The next, they were told to…

'Stop!' repeated the Sheriff. 'Do not harm those men. They are free to go!' He stood at the window above the castle's main door, but instead of his usual cruel expression, he looked pained. 'I have an announcement to make.' He cleared his throat noisily before beginning. 'I, Vaizey, Sheriff of Nottingham… in recognition of my illegal actions yesterday in Locksley… humbly apologise to the innocent people who suffered at my hand…'

While the Sheriff's men stared upwards in disbelief, Little John and the outlaws took their chance and began to move soundlessly towards the castle entrance. It was time to go.

'And I promise to pay…' prompted Robin, who stood with an arrow pointed at the Sheriff's neck just out of sight of the audience of guards.

'And I promise to pay…' Cringing with embarrassment, the Sheriff spoke in an undertone. 'No, enough! I would rather you *killed* me.' When there was no response, he turned to face his tormenter. But the room was empty – Robin had gone.

His blood boiling at the thought of how he

had been tricked, the Sheriff pointed at the departing outlaws. 'Guards! Here!' he cried furiously. 'Those men – get them! And Hood!'

CHAPTER ELEVEN

In the Sheriff of Nottingham's private chamber, a very strange thing was happening. The dead sentry, who lay on the floor with a feathered arrow protruding from his chest, suddenly opened one eye – and then the other eye. Finally, he sat bolt upright and removed his helmet.

It was Roy! Briefly, he smiled as he remembered the code word with which Robin had summoned him – Lavender. Well, perhaps Lavender Boy wasn't such a softy after all… He might even grow to like him.

By now, the rumpus in the courtyard had grown too loud to ignore – it was time for Roy to make his escape. In a trice, he was on his feet and away, the arrow in his chest wobbling dangerously as he ran. He hurtled through the

Sheriff's sumptuous quarters, then along bleak stone corridors, heading for the courtyard. As he ran, he tore away the guard's uniform. The tabard came off, revealing a block of splintered wood hanging around his neck – the arrow had not harmed him because it had struck the wooden armour instead!

Inwardly chuckling at the success of their cunning plan, Roy tossed the wood to once side before cannoning through the castle doors and sprinting down the steps towards the scrum of guards and outlaws.

At that moment, Robin was speeding along the battlements that ran along the edge of the courtyard. There was the gibbet before him. Thankfully, he spotted the arrow he'd fired earlier – its shaft had sunk far into the wooden frame and the rope dangled from it. Robin tugged the rope to make sure it held firm. It did. Now to secure the other end…

The fight in the courtyard had escalated into a full-scale brawl. Robin winced as he saw a guard land a punch on Forrest, but soon he spotted who he was looking for. 'Much!' he called. 'Tie this off!' He hurled the loose end of the rope to his faithful partner in crime.

Much caught the rope and then set about looking for somewhere to secure it. An iron ring would do. Or a sturdy post. Anything! But the courtyard appeared to be empty of such necessities.

'Here,' said Little John. He took the end of the rope, looped it around his body and planted himself firmly on the ground, his legs wide. *He* would be the anchor. The giant outlaw made eye contact with Robin, to signal that he was ready. Robin nodded gratefully. Then Little John turned to Much. 'You,' he said. 'Protect me.'

'Me?' Much couldn't believe that he was being trusted with such an important task. 'Oh… yes,' he said and obediently wielded his sword, putting his back to Little John in order to defend him.

High on the castle walls, Robin took a knife

and sliced through the bowstring of his trusty weapon, ready to begin his risky journey.

'On the battlements!' cried the Sheriff of Nottingham, pointing upwards. 'Shoot him!'

At once, two of his men took aim. But before they could fire, Will clouted them with his mighty wooden mace.

It was now or never. Robin hooked the curved bow over the rope and – his arms stretched wide – gripped either end. Then he launched himself into space, sliding faster and faster as he zoomed downhill towards Little John. Greedy fingers grabbed at him as he reached the bottom, but he kicked them out of the way before landing with an *oof* of relief.

At once, Robin found himself fighting back to back with Roy. 'That hurt, Lavender Boy!' he muttered under his breath, as he sliced his sword through the air.

'Heartbreaking,' said Robin, with a quick grin.

From the shadowy cloisters, Marian watched

Robin's heroic feat anxiously, relieved beyond measure to see him land safely. She shook her head, unaccustomed to such acts of bravery. Unable to look away, she stared as Robin's team – for they were clearly united – charged out of the courtyard. Their leader balanced precariously on a barrel to attack the enemy whilst the others escaped. When everyone was free, he slashed the rope holding open the portcullis, rolling beneath it just before the enormous gate came crashing to the ground.

They'd made it.

Robin of Locksley glanced back through the portcullis at the defeated Sheriff and his men, wearing a look of pure exhilaration on his face. Marian saw the look and she knew what it meant. The thrill of the fight – that was what made Robin feel alive. She couldn't beat that.

Suddenly, Robin spied her. He paused for a moment and blew her a gentle kiss. And then he was gone.

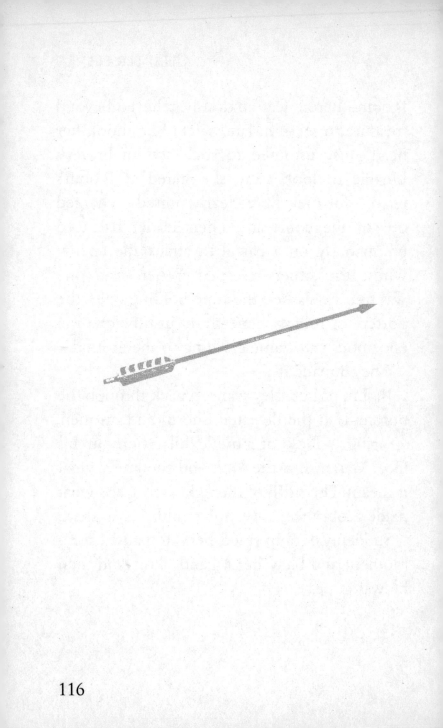

CHAPTER TWELVE

The morning sun shone brightly out of a clear sky, its light casting gentle shadows between the run-down houses. It was a new day – and a new village. Robin Hood and the outlaws waited a safe distance away, hidden among the dappled shadows of Sherwood Forest. They watched with keen eyes, as if searching for something… or someone.

Forrest gestured towards a young woman as she trudged out of a stable. She was so thin that he hardly recognised her and looked so weary that she might fall asleep on her feet.

'Her?' asked Little John.

Forrest nodded. It was, without doubt, his wife.

A short while later, the woman went to fetch her bucket. But in its place was a basket filled with meat, bread, fruit and nuts… more food than she'd seen for months. And there, nestling among the food, was a small purse. Tentatively, she took the purse and opened it. It contained two coins – a paltry sum for a Sheriff, but a small fortune for a hungry villager.

Forrest's wife looked around in disbelief. Who would do such a thing? Her eyes searched eagerly for her mysterious benefactor. But there was no one to be seen.

In Nottingham town, later that morning, a washerwoman plucked clothes from a line. It was the same job she did day in, day out. But today was different. As she unpegged a rough blanket, the woman revealed a purse lying on the ground – and beside it, a basket of precious food.

Roy watched the delight on his mother's face and he smiled to himself. Robin clapped him fondly on the back. Then, together, they disappeared.

That morning, breakfast was late in Sherwood Forest. Much, who was the keenest to eat, hungrily supervised the sizzling bacon and frying fish.

'I myself have no family, of course,' he murmured to the outlaws nearby. 'No family. No wife. No children. And surprisingly, it does not bother me – not at all.' A lone tear trickled down his cheek. Unconsciously, Much brushed it away. 'It does not bother me at all,' he repeated sadly.

Moments later, Little John returned sadly from his mission.

'Locksley?' Robin asked gently.

The outlaw nodded.

'All well?' added Robin.

Little John nodded again – the job was done. He gave a wan smile, brightening when he saw the delicious breakfast. Before the cook knew what was happening, Little John swiped the bacon from under his nose and happily sank his teeth into it.

'Hey, hey!' cried Much, outraged at this brazen

theft. 'I think you'll find that's not properly cooked!'

The outlaws exploded with laughter at the injured look on Much's face and the sounds of their merriment echoed throughout the leafy trees.

'Oh, very funny,' muttered Much. But, for once, even he could see the funny side and it wasn't long before he joined in.

Later that day, Little John made another trip to Locksley. He simply couldn't resist. He had to see with his own eyes that his wife and son were all right.

Robin accompanied him on the journey – Alice and the boy might be John's family, but they were his responsibility too. They were still his villagers.

Wearily, Alice and little Little John approached their house. The buckets they carried swayed from side to side, slopping water as they walked. But before they reached home, Alice stopped dead and stared in open-mouthed amazement.

Pinned to the doorframe was a pair of fishes. And lower down – at child height – hung a small boar ham. The little boy saw it and grinned.

Satisfied now that all was well, Little John turned to leave. Robin watched for a few moments longer before drawing his hood over his head and making his way back into Sherwood Forest.

Robin of Locksley, Earl of Huntingdon, was gone. He was Robin Hood now. He was an outlaw. And he had a job to do.

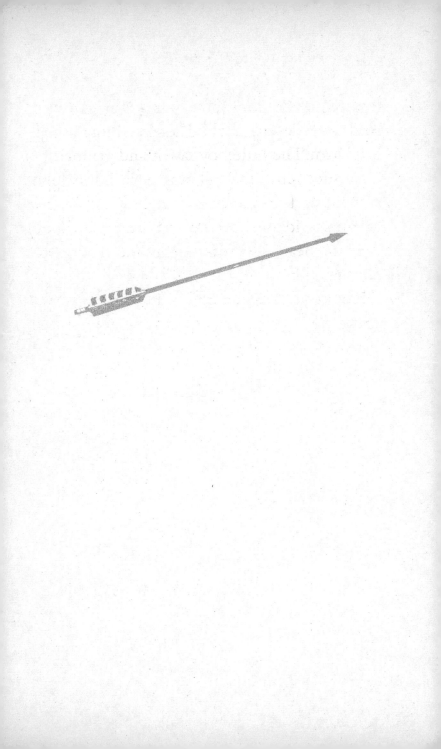